Sharon, Lois & Bram's

One Elephant
Went Out to Play

story by Randi Hampson

illustrated by Qin Leng

tundra

Come join us in the jungle
Where animals roam free

So we can share this song with you
'Neath the rain forest canopy.

Where a very special spider
Spins a web across the trees.

With drops of dew it glistens
And shimmers in the breeze.

And with the rising morning sun,
Her magic silk holds firm,

So she beckons to her special friend,
A playful pachyderm . . .

One elephant went out to play
Upon a spider's web one day.

She had such enormous fun
That she called for her baby elephant to come.

Two elephants went out to play
Upon a spider's web one day.

They had such enormous fun
That they called for a glamorous giraffe to come.

Three jungle friends went out to play
Upon a spider's web one day.

They had such enormous fun
That they called for a cranky crocodile to come.

Four jungle friends went out to play
Upon a spider's web one day.

They had such enormous fun
That they called for five little monkeys to come.

Nine jungle friends went out to play
Upon a spider's web one day.

They had such enormous fun
That they called for a silly, smiley snake to come.

1, 2,
3, 4, 5,
6, 7, 8,
9, 10

Ten jungle friends went out to play
Upon a spider's web one day.

They had such enormous fun
That they called for EVERYONE to come!

All the jungle friends were out at play
Upon a spider's web one day.

They had such enormous fun . . .

. . . that they'll be back tomorrow
when the new web's done!

SHARON HAMPSON, the late LOIS LILIENSTEIN (d. 2015) and BRAM MORRISON are some of Canada's most famous children's performers, with fans across North America and around the world. The trio, known simply as Sharon, Lois & Bram, formed in Toronto in 1978 and went on to create two top-rated children's television shows, *The Elephant Show* and *Skinnamarink TV*, and twenty-one full-length albums. Their songs feature silly animals, stories about friendship and themes of love. If you look closely, you can see characters from some of Sharon, Lois and Bram's most popular songs in this book! After Bram's retirement from touring in 2019 and with his enthusiastic support, Sharon and her daughter, **RANDI HAMPSON**, continue to entertain children and share their message of love through their music. You can find out more on www.sharonloisandbram.com or by following Sharon and Bram on social media @sharonloisbram.

QIN LENG has illustrated picture books, magazines and book covers with publishers around the world. Recent books include her author-illustrator debut *I Am Small*; *Ordinary, Extraordinary Jane Austen* written by Deborah Hopkinson; and *A Family Is a Family Is a Family* written by Sara O'Leary. Please visit www.qinillustrations.com.

This book is based on one of our most popular songs from our very first album, *One Elephant, Deux Éléphants*, and is inspired by our relationship with and enduring affection for elephants. We love doing the actions to this song where all the "elephants" join hands and are connected to each other. Now you can sing along with us and this new version of "One Elephant Went Out to Play," which can be found wherever you purchase music (look for the "All Friends Version"). We hope you also have fun searching for the fly on each page and discovering all of our animal friends! Keep up with our latest news on our socials @sharonloisbram. – S & B

To our King Spider, down the street. – Q

Text copyright © 2022 by Randi Hampson, Sharon Hampson, Lois Lilienstein and Bram Morrison
Illustrations copyright © 2022 by Qin Leng

Tundra Books, an imprint of Penguin Random House Canada Young Readers,
a division of Penguin Random House of Canada Limited

Library and Archives Canada Cataloguing in Publication

Title: Sharon, Lois and Bram's One elephant went out to play / story by Randi Hampson ; illustrations by Qin Leng.
Other titles: One elephant went out to play
Names: Hampson, Randi, author. | Leng, Qin, illustrator. | Sharon, Lois, and Bram.
Identifiers: Canadiana (print) 20210333057 | Canadiana (ebook) 20210333065 |
ISBN 9780735271081 (hardcover) | ISBN 9780735271098 (EPUB)
Classification: LCC PS8615.A5456 S52 2022 | DDC jC813/.6–dc23

Edited by Elizabeth Kribs
Designed by John Martz and Sophie Paas-Lang
The artwork in this book was created with ink and watercolor.
The text was set in Burbank Small.

Printed in China

www.penguinrandomhouse.ca

1 2 3 4 5   26 25 24 23 22

Penguin
Random House
TUNDRA BOOKS